WellieWishers™

The Rainstorm Brainstorm

By Valerie Tripp
Illustrated by Thu Thai

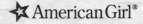
★ American Girl®

17 18 19 20 21 22 LEO 10 9 8 7 6 5 4 3 2 1

Editorial Development: Jodi Goldberg and Jennifer Hirsch
Art Direction and Design: Riley Wilkinson and Jessica Annoye
Production: Jeannette Bailey, Caryl Boyer, Lisa Bunescu, and Cynthia Stiles
Vignettes on pages 78-83 by Flavia Conley

For my dear friend,
Bea Dimichael

Meet the WellieWishers™

The WellieWishers are a group of fun-loving girls who each have the same big, bright wish: to be a good friend. They love to play in a large and leafy backyard garden cared for by Willa's Aunt Miranda.

Willa

Ashlyn

Emerson

When the WellieWishers step into their colorful garden boots, also known as wellingtons or *wellies*, they are ready for anything—stomping in mud puddles, putting on a show, and helping friendships grow. Like you, they're learning that being kind, creative, and caring isn't always easy, but it's the best way to make friendships bloom.

Kendall

Camille

Chapter 1

Birthday Countdown

*T*ap, tap, tap! *Tap, tap, tap!* Kendall happily tapped with her hammer. She and Willa had made a sign. It said:

Only 5 days until
Aunt Miranda's birthday!

"Aunt Miranda's birthday is coming!" said Willa.

"We'll have a party," said Ashlyn, her eyes sparkling.

"Let's start planning the party," said Kendall. She flipped open her notepad and held her pencil, ready to write. "What kind of cake shall we have?"

"Carrot cake," said Willa. "That's Aunt Miranda's favorite."

"And Carrot's, too, I bet," giggled Camille. She made up a little poem:

We'll celebrate with carrot cake
and happy songs and wishes.
We'll celebrate. It will be great!
We'll give her hugs and kisses.

"We'll have the party right here in the garden," said Ashlyn, "and there'll be pretty decorations like flowers and butterflies."

"And a big, beautiful present for Aunt Miranda!" added Emerson.

"A present!" cheered the girls.

Kendall flipped to a new page in her notebook. "What shall we give Aunt Miranda for a birthday present?" she asked.

"I know! I know!" said Ashlyn. "Let's give her decorations for the garden so that it looks like there's a party here every day!" Ashlyn sang to the tune of "Twinkle, Twinkle, Little Star":

Pretty decorations say,
"It's a party!" every day.

Willa had a different idea. "Aunt Miranda loves animals," she said. "The birthday present that she'd like best would be safe, cozy homes for the animals in the garden." Willa sang:

Homes for birds and
squirrels and skunks,
Made of wood or
in tree trunks.

"Homes for skunks?" said Emerson, wrinkling her nose. "No, the best present for Aunt Miranda is puppets. Then she could put on a show." Emerson pretended that her hands were a puppy puppet and a kitten puppet talking to each other, and she sang:

> *Puppy puppet says, "Bow-wow."*
> *Kitten puppet says, "Mee-yow."*

"Animal puppets are only pretend," said Camille. "Aunt Miranda would like *real* animals, something fancy, like a peacock or a dolphin." She sang:

Animals that swim and fly,
In the water, in the sky.

"I think Aunt Miranda would like something that she could *use* here in the garden," said Kendall. She sang:

How about a garden hose
Tied up with some pretty bows?

"I don't see how we can buy a hose," said Emerson. "We don't have any money. We could make puppets out of old socks for free."

"I still say she'd like a *real* animal," said Camille, picking up Carrot.

"She loves the animals that live here in the garden already," said Willa. "She'd like cozy homes for them."

"Stop!" said Ashlyn, holding up her hands. "We disagree about what we want Aunt Miranda's present to be. But we all agree on one thing."

"What?" asked her friends.

Ashlyn said, "We want her present to be GREAT!"

Chapter 2

The Tomorrow Pile

Suddenly, Carrot jumped out of Camille's arms. *Lickety-split, boingeddy-boing,* Carrot hippety-hopped away.

"Hey, where's Carrot going?" asked Camille.

Ribbit!

"Carrot's following that frog!" said Willa. "Let's see where they're headed."

The girls followed Carrot, who followed the frog through the tall grass. Suddenly, *plop*! The frog jumped into a jumble of old flowerpots and disappeared.

Carrot didn't mind. He found a cool, green clump of clover and settled down to snooze.

"What is all this stuff?" asked Emerson. With the toe of one wellie, she poked at a box.

"Aunt Miranda calls it the 'Tomorrow Pile,'" said Willa. "Some things are broken and need to be fixed, and other things need to be thrown away. She keeps saying that she's going to sort it out tomorrow, but she never gets to it."

"We could do it for her," said Kendall. "We could throw away the broken stuff and clear out the space. That would be a helpful present."

"You mean we'd give Aunt Miranda an empty space where a pile used to be?" said Camille. "That's a weird present."

"Besides, I don't want to touch that dirty old stuff," said Ashlyn. "I bet there are bugs and worms in that pile." She shuddered. "It's a mess."

But Kendall, who didn't mind messes, was already squatting next to the pile and carefully separating things. "Look at this," she said, holding up a dented mailbox and a muddy watering can. "We could repair these and give them to Aunt Miranda for her birthday present."

"I bet there are other things we could fix up in this pile, too," said Willa.

"Fixed-up stuff isn't as exciting as a dolphin," said Camille.

"True," agreed Kendall. "But at least it's something we could give her."

"And it's free," said Emerson.

"I think Kendall's idea is good," said Willa. "We'll be recycling, and Aunt Miranda likes that."

Kendall blew on the mailbox, and a cloud of dusty dirt rose from it. "We have some scrubbing to do before any of this stuff is clean enough for a

present, that's for sure."

Ashlyn stepped back. "This will be a messy job!" she said.

"You're right," said Kendall. "The messier, the better. I love messes!"

"It's a good thing we'll be wearing our wellies, in case we get wet," added Camille.

"Yes," agreed Emerson. "At least our feet will stay clean and dry!"

Chapter 3

Scrub-a-Dub-Dub

When the girls came to the old shed the next morning, they saw that Kendall had brought work gloves, scrub brushes, rags, and a bucket of sudsy, soapy water.

"Bubbles!" said Camille happily. "How fun!" She scooped up some soap bubbles and gently blew them into the air. "I like getting wet, so I'll do the scrubbing."

Willa said, "I'll help you scrub. We'll be scrub-a-dub-buddies." She churned up the sudsy water so that bubbles rose up into the air, catching the sunlight. When the bubbles drifted down, they popped with little kisses on Willa's arms.

Emerson tied Kendall's apron around her waist. "I'll cut the weeds and vines," she said. "Then you can pull things out of the pile, Kendall."

"Okay," said Kendall.

"I'll make a list of the things we might reuse," said Ashlyn, who didn't want to get too dirty. She picked up Kendall's pencil and notebook.

Emerson clipped and snipped. Willa and Camille scrubbed and rubbed. But as the sun rose higher, the day grew hotter, and Emerson's hands began to hurt from cutting vines and weeds. Camille and Willa had wrinkled, pruney fingers from washing.

Ashlyn was discouraged, because even after the things were washed, none of them looked like possible presents. There was an old spring, a flowerpot, pans, cans, rusty garden tools, and some pieces of wood. It all looked hopeless to her.

Ashlyn made a list of the things they had found. Then she slipped off to sit in the shade and began doodling in the notebook. She sketched flowers and flowerpots, leaves and hearts, swirls and smiley faces. She hummed to herself,

Pretty decorations say,
"It's a party!" every day.

Emerson swiped the sweat off her forehead. Cutting tangled-up weeds and twisted-up vines was hard work! "I need a break," she said to Kendall.

"Okay," Kendall mumbled. She was knee-deep in the Tomorrow Pile, tugging on a spring that was caught in vines.

Emerson took off the apron, draped it over her shoulders like a cape, and tied the strings in a bow under her chin. She held the scissors as if they were a microphone and danced over to join Ashlyn in the shade, singing:

Puppy puppet says, "Bow-wow." Kitten puppet says, "Mee-yow."

Camille caught the spirit of silliness. She put on Kendall's safety goggles and said, "Look at me, I'm a deep-sea diver!" Then she picked up Kendall's hammer and swam it through the air, saying, "I found a seahorse!" She swished and swooped over to the shade to join Ashlyn and Emerson, singing:

Animals that swim and fly.
In the water, in the sky.

Willa grinned. Camille was right: The hammer *did* look like a sea horse. Willa held up Kendall's tape measure. "This looks just like a giant ladybug," she said. "I'm going to make a terrarium for it." Willa joined the other girls in the shade, singing:

> *Homes for birds and*
> *squirrels and skunks,*
> *Made of wood or in tree trunks.*

All of a sudden, the spring sprang free from the vines and Kendall fell backward, *boink!*

"Look!" she said breathlessly, holding up the spring. "I got it!"

But no one answered. Everyone was too busy playing with Kendall's tools in the shade of the big, leafy tree.

Chapter 4

No Tools?
No Present.
No Fooling!

The next morning, the girls were back in the garden, singing merrily to the tune of "I'm a Little Teapot":

We're the WellieWishers,
We like fun,
Here in the garden,
Under the sun.

We love Aunt Miranda,
Soon we'll say:
"It's your birthday,
Hip-hip, hooray!"

"Did you hear our song, Kendall?" asked Ashlyn.

"Isn't it *wonderful?*" said Emerson. "Don't you *love* it?"

Kendall didn't answer. She just sat on the bench looking gloomy.

Camille sat down next to Kendall. "What's the matter?" she asked.

"The song is right," said Kendall. "Aunt Miranda's birthday is soon. But we don't have a present for her."

"You mean, we don't have one *yet*," said Ashlyn.

"We might *never* have one," said Kendall.

"Never?" asked the girls in surprise. "What do you mean?"

"I can't find my tools," said Kendall.

"We need my tools to make the stuff from the Tomorrow Pile into presents."

"Uh-oh," the other girls said, looking sheepishly at one another.

"Sorry, Kendall," said Ashlyn. "We were playing, and then it was time to go home, and I guess we forgot and left your tools under the tree."

"We'll go and get them right now," said Emerson. "Come on, girls."

Off they rushed to the shady tree. It had rained in the night, so the ground under the tree was wet, and fallen sticks and leaves had glommed together. The girls had to search on their hands and knees, looking for Kendall's tools where they'd dropped them. It was hard to find them, because the tools blended in so well with the sticks and leaves. When at last they had found all the tools, they ran back to Kendall and put the tools on the bench next to the playhouse.

"Here you go," said Willa.

Kendall didn't say anything. She didn't need to say anything, because her face showed how upset she was. And it was easy to see why:

Kendall's hammer was dirty.

Her pencil was blunt.

Her apron was wrinkled.

Her goggles were smoggy.

Her tape measure was tangled.

Her scissors were gummy.

Her notepad was a soggy mess.

Kendall's tools looked as terrible as the stuff in the Tomorrow Pile.

"Sorry," said Emerson in a small voice.

"*Sorry?*" asked Kendall. Her voice was tight and tearful. "We were supposed to be working all together. But you quit working to go off and play," she said to her friends. "You used my tools as toys. Then you left them out in the rain, and now they are muddy and messy and ruined. I can't use my tools when they're like this," Kendall said. "No one can. You can forget about making a present for Aunt Miranda. So now you've ruined her birthday, too." Then Kendall stomped away.

"Whoa," whispered Willa. No one had ever seen Kendall so upset before. The WellieWishers felt ashamed.

"Come on," said Camille. She started picking up Kendall's mucky tools and said, "We've got some work to do."

"No fooling," said Emerson.

Chapter 5

Brainstorm in a Rainstorm

Plip, plop, drip, drop. Rain pitter-pattered on Kendall's umbrella as she came to the garden the next morning. When she looked up, she was surprised to see her friends already there, waiting for her. Camille, Emerson, Ashlyn, and Willa sang to the tune of "I'm a Little Teapot":

We are very sorry.
Hear our song:
We left your tools out,
That was wrong.
Now we will return them,
Good as new.
Please forgive us,
Kendall, do.

Willa held out her hand. "Come with us, Kendall," she said. "We have something to show you."

Kendall took Willa's hand, and in a soggy parade, the WellieWishers

splish-sploshed their way to the playhouse. Mud splashed up on the backs of their legs, and rain fell outside their umbrellas like a gray curtain.

"Oh!" gasped Kendall when they went inside the playhouse. Her friends had washed, dried, and polished the stuff from the Tomorrow Pile and lined it up along the wall. Kendall's tools were laid out neatly on the table.

Kendall stepped toward the table. She hardly recognized her tools. Her friends had not only cleaned them— they had transformed them!

The handle of her hammer was painted with jazzy stripes.

The new cover of her notepad was decorated with ladybugs and flowers.

Her tape measure was painted to look like a ladybug.

The frames of her safety goggles were shiny clean, and even her pencil had a pretty blue tip to match her scissors.

"Oh, oh, oh," said Kendall, gently touching her hammer and her ladybug tape measure. "How did you do this? My tools look better than ever."

"And that's not all," announced Emerson. "Ta-da!" Emerson whisked Kendall's apron out from behind her back. "Don't you *love* it? Isn't it *won*derful?"

"Yes!" said Kendall, beaming. The apron was the most tremendous transformation of all. The girls had added cheery rickrack to the bottom hem and, best of all, a big, flowery pocket to hold Kendall's tools.

Emerson tied the apron around Kendall's waist. Willa put Kendall's scissors, pencil, notebook, and safety goggles in the big pocket. Camille hung Kendall's hammer in its special holder.

"There!" said Ashlyn. "Now you have the world's cutest tool belt!"

"Thank you," said Kendall, admiring her new apron and decorated tools.

"You're welcome," said the girls.

"We're sorry that we messed up your tools," said Emerson. "Do you forgive us?"

"Oh, yes," said Kendall wholeheartedly. "I love my tools and my apron. But—" She paused. "There is one thing that would make them even *more* wonderful."

"What?" asked the girls.

"This," said Kendall, handing her hammer to Camille, her scissors to Emerson, her notebook and pencil to Ashlyn, and her tape measure to Willa.

"Now my tools are perfect—because we're all using them together."

"Hooray!" Willa said, waving the ladybug tape measure as if it were cheering. "Let's go measure something!"

"Yes!" laughed Camille, making the hammer swim through the air like a seahorse. "I'll come with you!"

Emerson picked up the mailbox and opened its door like a big mouth. "Me, too," she said to the ladybug and sea-horse, as if the mailbox were talking.

Ashlyn laughed. "They're almost like puppets," she exclaimed.

Kendall shouted, "That's it!"

The other girls looked at Kendall. The only sound was the *rat-a-tat* of the rain on the roof.

"I've had a brainstorm," said Kendall.

"A *brainstorm*?" asked Camille.

"Yes!" said Kendall. "You've shown me how we can give Aunt Miranda all the things we want to give her."

"How?" asked the other girls.

Kendall said, "You decorated my tools to make them pretty, like art, and now we can also play with them, like toys. Well, what if we do that with the stuff from the Tomorrow Pile? We could paint it and make it into fun stuff to look at, or play with—"

"Like animals," Camille burst in.

"Or homes for animals," said Willa.

"With pretty decorations," added Ashlyn.

"Or like puppets!" exclaimed Emerson, opening and shutting the mailbox again as if it were a mouth. "Right?" she made the mailbox say.

"Right!" laughed Kendall. "*Now* you're talking!" And all five girls ran to the pile of stuff and began choosing things to make for Aunt Miranda.

Chapter 6

Happy Birthday, Aunt Miranda!

On the big day, Willa rang Aunt Miranda's doorbell, and when she opened the door, the girls sang:

Happy birthday to you,
Happy birthday to you,
Happy birthday, Aunt Miranda,
Happy birthday to you!

"Thank you for singing to me," said Aunt Miranda.

"We have birthday presents for you, too," said Ashlyn.

"But they're not the kind you unwrap," said Camille.

"You'll *love* them," gushed Emerson. "They're *won*derful."

"Come with us," said Kendall, and the WellieWishers led Aunt Miranda to her first present.

"Aunt Miranda, we know how much you love all the animals that live here in the garden," said Willa. "So I thought that you'd like a cozy home for some of them." She added jokingly, "This home's for the birds."

"What a beautiful birdhouse," said Aunt Miranda. "I'm sure that the birds in the garden will love it as much as I do. Thank you, Willa."

"Oh, I didn't make it by myself," said Willa. "We all worked together."

"All of us worked together on *my* idea, too," said Ashlyn. She tugged on Aunt Miranda's hand, pulling her farther along the garden path. "I wanted the garden to look all ready for a party, so we made these decorations."

"Oh, how lovely!" said Aunt Miranda. "They're perfect for a party."

"Wait till you see *my* idea!" said Emerson, skipping backward as the girls led Aunt Miranda to the stage. "These are more decorations for the garden," said Emerson. "But guess what? We made them look like a kitty and a puppy!"

"Bravo!" clapped Aunt Miranda. "I love garden art, and I love animals. And these are both!"

"My present is an animal, too," said Camille. "It's over here." Camille and the other girls led Aunt Miranda to the shady tree. "Now, watch."

Whooosh! Camille blew as hard as she could, and the weather-vane chicken spun around.

Aunt Miranda clapped with delight. "Now I'll always know which way the wind is blowing," she said. "That's a very helpful chicken!"

"My present is also helpful," said Kendall. "Would you like to see?"

"Yes, please," said Aunt Miranda.

"Then follow me," said Kendall.

The other girls giggled as Kendall led Aunt Miranda to the old shed.

"At first, I wanted to give you a garden hose," said Kendall. "But I think this signpost that we made will be just as useful and helpful as a hose."

"I think so, too," agreed Aunt Miranda. "If visitors are walking through the garden, this signpost will help them if they're wondering which path to take." She smiled. "Now I am curious: Where on earth did you get the materials to make all these great gifts?"

"You'll see!" laughed Kendall as she led Aunt Miranda around to the back of the shed. "We used stuff from the Tomorrow Pile to make the presents," said Kendall. "See? Your pile is all gone."

"Oh, my goodness!" exclaimed Aunt Miranda. "Thank you for clearing out that pile of old stuff for me—that's a great present, too! The pile is gone, the stuff in the pile was reused, and I love the presents that you all worked together to make for me."

Then the WellieWishers sang:

Happy birthday to you,
Happy birthday to you,
Happy birthday, Aunt Miranda,
Every day we love you!

Aunt Miranda smiled. "This is an *altogether* great birthday," she said.

"Thanks to Kendall's rainstorm brainstorm!" laughed the WellieWishers, all together.

For Parents

DIY Decluttering

Much like Aunt Miranda, you might sometimes find that clutter is piling up. Instead of tackling another dull cleanup chore on your own (or putting it off until tomorrow), invite your girl to help turn a "tomorrow pile" of discards into a trove of unexpected treasures. Here's how:

Mom's Thrift Shop

The next time you clean out your closet, invite your girl to try on some of the clothes that you're getting rid of. She'll have a kick playing dress-up. Spice things up with a mini fashion show, and narrate with your best announcer voice.

Garden Makeover

Do you have a bunch of plastic pots that have seen better days? Give old planters a makeover! Clean and paint a plastic pot with primer, and then let your girl decorate it with her own designs. Lay out water-based acrylic, tempera, or poster paints in bright colors, along with a variety of brushes, stencils, and sponges to paint with.

Treasure Tins

If your girl has knickknacks and small toys that clutter her room, help her transform old popcorn, candy, and mint tins into keepsake boxes with colored paper, stickers, and washi tape. She'll love creating her own containers for her small stuff, and you can teach her about tidying up.

Rotating Art Wall

Create a rotating art gallery of your girl's masterpieces. Fill old frames with pieces of foam core or cardboard, and mount her latest creations with glue dots or repositionable glue stick. Hang the frames in your daughter's room, play area, or the family room for all to admire!

Clean It Out!

When it's time to get rid of unused or worn-out items instead of upcycling them, your girl can help. Bring her along to your community's donation center. Explain to her that other people will be glad to have your unwanted clothes and will make good use of them.

Or if you'd rather have a rummage sale, let her
help by setting out (and perhaps having one last
play session with) her old toys and outfits she's
outgrown. You can share stories and memories
about the items as she displays them. On the day
of the sale, let her run her own little enterprise
with a lemonade stand.

About the Author

VALERIE TRIPP says that she became
a writer because of the kind of person she is.
She says she's curious, and writing requires you
to be interested in everything. Talking is her
favorite sport, and writing is a way of talking
on paper. She's a daydreamer, which helps her
come up with her ideas. And she loves words.
She even loves the struggle to come up
with just the right words as she writes
and rewrites. Ms. Tripp lives in
Maryland with her husband.